The Ring Bear

A RASCALLY WEDDING ADVENTURE

Written by David Michael Slater

Illustrated by S.G. Brooks

Flashlight Press

New York

J
E
C.I

For Zach, Molly, Naava, Julia, Audrey, Ryan, Ross, Emma and especially MAX. –DMS

For Terri, a longtime friend and teacher, in appreciation of your encouragement
and support. I hope this is a special addition to your bear collection. –SGB

Copyright © 2004 by Flashlight Press
Text copyright © 2004 by David Michael Slater
Illustrations copyright © 2004 by S.G. Brooks

Library of Congress Control Number: 2003116498

ISBN 0-972-92251-2

Editor: Shari Dash Greenspan
Graphic Design: The Virtual Paintbrush
This book was typeset in New Baskerville.
Illustrations were rendered in gouache, acrylic and black colored pencil
on Strathmore Bristol Vellum.

Distributed by Independent Publishers Group

Flashlight Press • 3709 13th Avenue • Brooklyn, NY 11218
www.FlashlightPress.com

"Ahoy Captain!"

Mom shouted to Westley while swabbing the decks. Westley the Wicked and Mom the Mean were the most dreaded pair of pirates on the seven seas.

"All hands on deck!" Captain Westley roared. "Me-thinks a storm's a brewin'!"

"Shiver me timbers," said Mom the Mean, "Is it a big one?"

"Nothin' a couple of rascally pirates like us can't handle, Matey!"

"Aye, Aye, Captain!"

Mom's friend Stan came aboard sometimes too, though he refused
to wear an eye patch and wouldn't search for stowaways.
Westley didn't mind too much – as long as Stan knew he was
only a guest of the crew. Guests didn't get pirate names.
That was Captain's Rule
Number One.

One day, right in the middle of digging for buried treasure, Mom the Mean took off her hook and said, "Avast, Captain, I've got somethin' important to tell ye. Stan and I are going to be married – and we want you to be our ring bearer!"

Westley tried to smile, but then dropped his shovel, abandoned his treasure and staggered back to his ship.

"Ring bearrrr?!" he thundered, feeling marooned.
"She wants me to be a bear? ARRRR!"

Then Westley threw down his patch and rumbled,
"If I have to be a bear, I'll be a rascally one! GRRRR!"

That evening, Stan brought flowers for Mom. Westley snatched them, and when he snuck away, thick, woolly fur grew on his arms and chest, and his hands became paws with long, sharp claws!

Stan's picture was next. When Westley hid it, fur covered his face and feet. He grew real bear ears and a real bear snout!

He really was the rascally Ring Bear now!

To be as frightening as possible, the Ring Bear yanked off his clothes. Then he crept up behind Mom and Stan.

He grrr'ed viciously...

Outraged, the Ring Bear
went and scuttled his ship...

...and turned his room
into a bear cave.

For the next few weeks, while his Mom was busy with wedding plans, Westley stayed in his cave imagining all the ways he could wreck the wedding. He'd snatch up the flowers and chew them to bits. He'd gnash his teeth and growl at the guests. He'd swallow the cake down in one beary bite.

Whenever Westley's mom had a moment to look in on him she asked if something was wrong, but the Ring Bear was too busy to answer.

The big day arrived all too soon and the backyard brimmed with eager guests. But the Ring Bear, crammed into his tuxedo, huddled alone in his cave.

He wished he could hibernate for the rest of his life. Finally, Mom and Stan peeked in on him. "Are you finished changing yet?" Mom asked.

"GRRRR! You can't change me," Westley snarled. "I'm already the Ring Bear! I'm rotten and vicious and nasty and mean, and I'll scare everyone away with one mighty

Rooooaaaaarrrr!"

"Oh, Mr. Bear," Mom said softly, "I'm so sorry, but we were hoping for a ring bearER. That's a boy, a special boy like Westley, who's chosen to carry the wedding rings. Mr. Bear, could you tell Westley how much I want him to carry the rings for us? We can't have a perfect wedding without our most important guest."

"And Mr. Bear, could you please tell Westley that I love him more than anything in the world?"

Confused, the Ring Bear lumbered to the backyard. The wedding had started and it was Westley's turn to walk down the aisle. But the Ring Bear couldn't move.

He could only stare down at the two shiny rings in his grizzly paws. Westley knew his mom loved him. But what about Stan?

"You're still a rascally Ring Bear!" a growly voice grumbled in his head. "You can gobble up these rings and chase everyone away!"

All the guests were watching and waiting.

The Ring Bear licked his lips and opened his mouth to gobble the rings.

Just then a pirate called out,
"Blimey, Captain, there's a bear stowed away
on our ship!" Westley looked up. The pirate
was Stan – and he was wearing an eye patch!

Suddenly Westley
charged down the aisle shouting,
"YOU'LL WALK THE PLANK, BEAR!"
With each step, his fur, claws and paws disappeared.

When he handed the rings to Mom and Stan, the Ring Bear vanished completely.

"I'm so glad yer back, Captain," Mom whispered. "Do you think the Ring Bear is gone for good?"

"Aye, that he is," the Captain replied. "But if that hairy land-lubber ever tries to board me ship again, he'll have to deal with Westley the Wicked!"

"Ahoy!" cried Mom, "not to mention Mom the Mean."

"Ahoy!" cried Captain Westley. "And don't forget Stan – Stan the… Stan the… Sort of Scary?"

"Ahoy!" cried Stan.
"Ahoy!" cried Westley, "All hands
on deck! Gang way for the most terrible
trio of pirates on the seven seas!"